P9-CFG-451

• RETOLD BY •

ALAN SCHROEDER

• ILLUSTRATED BY •

ANDREW GLASS

CLARION BOOKS
New York

Clarion Books
a Houghton Mifflin Company imprint
215 Park Avenue South, New York, NY 10003

The Tale of Willie Monroe is an adaptation of a Japanese folktale dating from the thirteenth century. Two spirited retellings of this story are Claus Stamm's *Three Strong Women* (Viking, 1962) and Irene Hedlund's *Mighty Mountain and the Three Strong Women* (Volcano Press, 1990). In both books, a powerful Japanese wrestler hopes to win the Emperor's Wrestling Match. On his way to the contest, however, he encounters three exceptionally strong women, who spend the next three months training him for success.

The illustrations for this book were executed in oil paint and colored pencil on paper.
The text is set in 14/19-point Caslon.

Printed in Singapore.

LIBRARY OF CONGRESS CATALOGING-IN-PUBLICATION DATA

Schroeder, Alan.
The tale of Willie Monroe / by Alan Schroeder ; illustrated by Andrew Glass.
p. cm.
Summary: An adaptation, set in the American South, of an old Japanese folktale in which a powerful wrestler who hopes to win the Emperor's Wrestling Match encounters three exceptionally strong women who train him for success.
ISBN 0-395-69852-9
[1. Folklore—Japan.] I. Glass, Andrew, 1949– ill. II. Title.
PZ8.1.S37Tal 1999
[398.2]–dc20
[E] 96-22493
CIP
AC

TWP 10 9 8 7 6 5 4 3 2 1

To Fred and Dorothy Gydesen
—A.S.

To Taylor Tecumseh Glass
—A.G.

One time, way back, there was this real big feller named Willie Monroe—strongest critter in all of Tennessee. Arms as big as stovepipes and a chest as broad as a barn door.

"I can whip ye with both hands tied behin' my back," he'd boast. And taking one look at him, neighbor-folks reckoned he was speaking the truth.

One morning, Willie was walking down the road when he saw a notice stuck up on a pole. Now, Willie, he couldn't read so good—was right grateful, then, when a crow flew down and offered to make out the wording for him.

" 'Pears to be a contest," said the bird, staring hard at the lettering. "An arm-wrestlin', log-stackin', cow-milkin', field-plowin', barn-raisin' contest. Says here, the person who can do all that, and do it the fastest, gets a big ol' bag o' money and ten acres of free land."

Well, right then and there, Willie figured he'd enter that contest. Made himself a journey cake and off he went, heading toward Carolina.

After a while, he started singing out loud to pass the time:

"Oh Lulu! Oh Lulu! Oh Lulu my dear!
I'd give the whole world if my Lulu was here!"

Willie walked on, walked on. Sun's a-shining, and Willie, he starts feeling a mite tired. Just then, he saw this little girl a-coming toward him, balancing a bucket on her head. Now, Willie, he could be the mischievous type. Figured he'd tip over that bucket, just for the fun of it.

"It won't do her no harm," he said with a chuckle. "And I'll refill it afterwards, just t' be nice."

But Willie was in for a shock. Soon as he stuck out his big ol' finger, the girl brought down her arm, trapping his hand.

"Hey thar!" Willie yelped. "What d'you think yer doin'?"

"That's what ye git for tryin' to trick me," said the girl, all smiles. "My name's Delilah. What's yers?"

"You better let go," said Willie. "Else I might hurt ye accident'ly when I pull away."

"I'd like to see that," said the girl. "Go on 'n' try."

Now, Willie, he begins a-pulling, just a little bit at first, then a little more and a little more. Didn't do a bit of good. His hand was stuck to stay.

"Let go o' me!" he cried. "Yer hurtin'!" And Willie, he couldn't believe he was saying that—not to a little girl, anyhow.

"Where ye off to?" said Delilah, continuing on down the road.

"You wouldn't know nothin' 'bout it," said Willie, stumbling after. "There's this arm-wrestlin', log-stackin', cow-milkin', field-plowin', barn-raisin' contest, and I'm gonna win it."

"Oh, I know all 'bout that contest," Delilah told him. "My granny, she won it two years ago. Set a record, too, for the cow-milkin' portion. Milked twenty-eight cows in two and a half minutes."

Willie, he snickered, figuring the poor girl'd been out in the sun too long.

"It's the truth," said Delilah. "Wait till you meet m' granny—you'll see."

By then, they were starting to climb a hill.

"Come on now," said Delilah, "pick up yer feet. Yer walkin' awful slow. If yer tired, I kin carry ye."

"I ain't tired!" Willie retorted. "Now let go o' me. I don't have time to be foolin' with the likes o' you."

But Delilah, she just smiled sweetly and shook her head.

"Seein' as how I like ye," she said, "I'm gonna help ye win that contest. 'Course, me an' my granny, we gotta get ye strengthened up first. Why, look at ye—one good wind'd blow ye right over the rooftop. Didn't yer mama ever feed ye?"

Willie, he just gave up at that point. Stumbled along with a face redder than a summer tomato.

A bit later, after passing through a heap of brush, the two of them reached Delilah's cabin. Only then did she release Willie's hand.

"Now don't ye be runnin' off," she warned. "I'll set m' granny on ye, and she'll outrun ye in two seconds flat."

Just then, the ground beneath their feet started to shake something awful.

"HIT'S A SOIL-JIGGLER!" Willie hollered.

But Delilah, she knew it wasn't an earthquake. She just pointed up the ridge a ways, and looking up, Willie saw this old granny-woman a-coming toward them, a full-grown horse slung over her shoulders. Every step the old lady took set the ground a-quivering.

"That's m' granny," said Delilah. "Jest look at 'er—don't she get around good for ninety-nine?"

The old lady, she came up, set the horse down gentle, then wiped her hands on her apron.

"Poor thing," she said to Delilah, pointing at the horse. "Got a rock caught in his shoe and couldn't take but hardly a step. Had to carry him clear from Onion River—twenty-five mile, I reckon. 'Course, he didn't weigh nothin' to speak of, but still, it's a awful nuisance." Then, turning to one side, the old lady noticed Willie standing there.

"Who's this puny li'l feller?" she asked.

"I found him on the road," said Delilah. "He's headin' for the arm-wrestlin', log-stackin', cow-milkin', field-plowin', barn-raisin' contest. You remember—the one I won last year. Thinks he's gonna win all that money an' ten acres o' land."

Reaching over, Granny squeezed one of Willie's muscles.

"Why mister," she grunted, "yer as weak as water! I bet ye couldn't pick up m' horse, even if ye was tryin'. No, sirree. We're gonna have to feed ye plenty of vittles and get ye some proper exercise if you're gonna win that contest. Tell me, what's yer name?"

Willie puffed out his chest real wide. "Willie Monroe," he boasted, "strongest critter in Tennessee."

"Well, come on in, Willie. Me 'n' my granddaughter, we'll do what we can t' toughen you up."

"I'm tough enough already," Willie muttered.

As she was turning to go inside, the old granny-woman tripped over a stump sticking out of the ground.

"Well, blast it!" she declared, picking herself up. "Third time this week I done tripped over that thing. That tree stump's gotta go!" And, bending down, she ripped it right out of the ground, roots and all. Taking aim, she threw the heavy stump clear up the mountainside. Made this little crashing sound way off in the distance. "Blast it!" Granny said again, massaging her shoulder. "I meant to throw it *over* the ridge. I tell you, sonny, it's awful bein' ninety-nine."

But Willie, he couldn't answer. He'd fainted dead away.

Next day, come sunrise, Granny and Delilah served Willie a hearty breakfast—twenty-five eggs, thirty pieces of bacon, sixteen glasses of juice, and over a dozen buttermilk pancakes.

"I realize it ain't much," said Granny, "but if you can finish all that, I'll fix ye a proper breakfast tomorrow. This here's just a morsel, to git ye started."

After vittle-time, they went outside to begin Willie's training.

"When we're done with ye," Granny promised, "you'll be the strongest feller in all o' Carolina."

"I'm already the strongest feller in Tennessee," said Willie, but Delilah and Granny pretended not to hear.

"First," said Delilah, "we gotta toughen up yer stomach muscles, then yer leg muscles, then yer arm muscles. Why don't ye try liftin' that lumber wagon a couple hundred times? Granny does it ever' mornin', just to git limbered up."

Willie tried, but he couldn't get the wagon to budge. Tried every day for a week—finally got to the point where he could lift one wheel, but that was all.

Granny tisked her tongue, real sad-like.

"It's a sorry sight to see," she said. "Big feller lak you as weak as a daisy. But I reckon it ain't fair to criticize ye too much, seein' as how you must'a been the runt o' yer family."

Even so, Granny wasn't about to make it easy for Willie. Every morning, before the sun was up, she'd have him chopping wood and toting water and digging ditches and repairing fences till he was panting like a shaggy dog on a summer day.

After the second week, Willie's muscles were a bit tougher, but not much.

"Do ye think we'll get him ready in time?" asked Delilah.

Granny frowned. "It's hard to say. We'll just have t' do the best we can."

Willie, he'd never worked so hard in all his life. Every night, soon as his head hit the pillow, he was out like a light.

"Look at 'im," said Granny. "Sleepin' just like a baby. Can ye imagine, after that li'l bitty bit o' work he done today, to be that tired? Delilah, we'd better start workin' him double hard, or he's never gonna win that contest."

Next day, come sunup, Granny pointed to a barrel of nails.

"I have a task for ye, Willie. I want ye to take them nails 'n' hammer down the roof o' the henhouse. It blowed loose in the last storm."

"I shore will." Willie glanced around. "Whar's the hammer?"

Granny just stared.

"Don't tell me ye need a hammer?" she sighed. "Sakes alive, use yer fists!"

That sounded awful painful to Willie, but turned out that pounding them nails was right good exercise—toughened up his hands till they were hard as rocks. Before, when he'd crack his knuckles, it sounded like a walnut splitting in two. Now, when he'd crack them, it sounded like a clap of thunder racing across the sky.

Granny and Delilah fed Willie the heartiest vittles, and every evening after supper he'd have to wrestle with one of them, most often with Granny.

"She bein' weaker than me," Delilah explained, "she's less likely to hurt ye. 'Sides, it's good for her rheumatiz."

So every night, Willie and Granny would wrestle around in the dirt, kicking up a fearsome cloud of dust.

Of course, at first Granny was always pinning him down, and that was awful shameful for Willie, seeing as how she only used one hand when she was wrestling with him.

Then, one day, Willie actually held her down for more than ten seconds.

"Yer gettin' purty strong," said Granny, after she'd thrown him off. "I reckon yer 'bout ready for that contest. But let's give it another week, just to make sure. No sense a-rushin' nature."

The following night, Willie met Delilah out by the pea patch. The moon was shining bright, and Delilah had never looked so pretty as she did standing there, with a sprig of dogwood stuck in her hair. Willie, he came straight to the point.

“I love ye,” he said, “and when I come back, I wanna marry ye. Think yer Granny’ll mind?”

“That depends,” said Delilah. “If you win, she’ll be right proud to have you in the family. But if ye lose . . . well, I reckon she’ll say no. One time, a year back, this feller named Bunyan come by, askin’ for my hand in marriage, and Granny, she run him off the property. Claimed he warn’t man enough. So, don’t ye see, Willie? You just got t’ win that contest.”

A week later, bright and early, Willie took a basket of journey cakes and started off toward Carolina. He walked on, walked on. Finally arrived at the field where the contest was being held. Everywhere Willie looked, there were big men strutting around, all boasting about how strong they were.

"Anytime my horse needs a-shoein'," said one feller, "I just flop 'im over on my lap and shoe 'im that way."

"That's nothin'," said another. "My li'l missy, she got right tired walkin' four miles to the river every day for water, so I just grabbed me one end o' that river and pulled it right up to our doorstep. They don't call me the strongest feller in Alabama for nothin'!"

Willie, he didn't say a word. Just sat down on a bench and waited till it was time for the contest to begin.

The arm-wrestling portion came first. Willie, he stepped up to the table, and *whack, whack, whack,* he wrestled down a dozen arms faster than the judges could count. *Whack! whack! whack!* Bent down ten more, just for show.

"Yer a trickster!" declared one of the fellers who'd been beat. "I dare ye to do it again." So Willie did, just to show that he wasn't cheating.

Upon seeing that, half the men suddenly recollected they had to be somewhere else right quick. Took off down the road faster than you can say "scat!" to a cat. The other half who stayed—well, they looked *mighty* worried.

By then, it was time for the log-stacking portion.

"On yer mark," said the judge, "git set . . . commence!"

Men started scrambling like crazy, throwing one log up on top of another. But Willie, he worked faster than them all. In five minutes flat he had a stack higher than a barn roof. Same thing

for the cow-milking, field-plowing, and barn-raising portions. Ol' Willie, he plowed twenty-seven acres in three and a half minutes. Had everyone's jaw just a-dropping.

By the end of the contest, all the strong men were standing around, moaning and griping, using words that ain't fit to tell. But Willie paid them no mind. He knew he'd won fair and square.

The head judge came swaggering forward with a big medal in his hand.

"Yer one tough fella," he said, pinning the medal on Willie's chest. "How'd ye get so strong?"

"A li'l girl 'n' her granny showed me how," Willie said.

Everyone burst out laughing, but Willie didn't care because he knew he was speaking the truth.

Then, swinging the bag of money over his shoulder, he set off down the road. Didn't take him but two days to reach Delilah's cabin, seeing as how every step he took covered nearly two yards. That's how excited he was.

Granny and Delilah were waiting for him out on the porch.

"Well?" said Granny. "Did they lick ye or not?"

Willie, he just beamed.

"Hope you got a dress all prepared," he told Delilah, "'cause there's gonna be a weddin'." And he held up the bag of money and the property-owning papers to the land.

"I knew you'd win!" Delilah cried, and she started dancing a jig so hard, it caused the whole cabin to tilt to one side.

Willie and Delilah were married the following spring, and to this day, Willie still wrestles with Granny, kicking up a fearsome cloud of dust. 'Course, Granny's more than a hundred now, but it don't hurt her none.

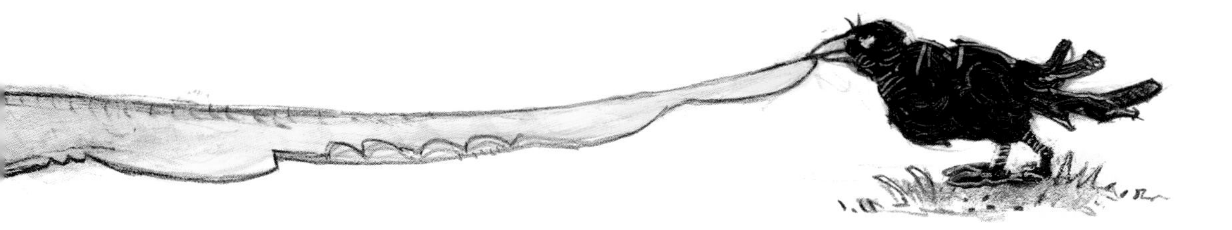

Besides, it's good for her rheumatiz.

THE END